PATCHES
The Cow Dog

Elizabeth I. Acree

Illustrations by Nancy Nehls Nelson

To all the wonderful beings in this world
and the inspiring relationships they form.

And with grateful thanks to Anne Jordan.

Deep in the countryside,

there lived a man

whom everyone there in the

little town called Mr. B.

He had a real name

but no one ever remembered it.

Everyone just called him Mr. B.

Mr. B had a big herd of cattle and his
cattle lived on the levee. A levee is a
big ol' hill, sort of, that runs right
alongside the mighty river.
It flows through the countryside there.
Near this river and this little town
was a big old farm.
It had a big, rambling house on it.
Lots of the people from the town
worked there for their living.
These townspeople were all friends of Mr. B.

Mr. B. also had a beautiful horse
whom he called Doubletime.
He called her that because she had a
sweet little quick step called a gait.
The gait made her make double time
when she walked. So, Mr. B had named her
Doubletime when he got her, many years ago.
He loved Doubletime very much.

Now every day, twice a day,

Mr. B would ride Doubletime through

his herd of cows up on the levee.

He did this to check on his cows, to make sure

everything was alright with them.

One day, while riding, Mr. B saw something

white and round dart out in front of him

and then disappear. Mr. B couldn't make out

what it was. Doubletime pricked up her ears

and pointed them straight ahead, for she

had seen it, too. "Let's go see what that was,

Doubletime," Mr. B said. So, Doubletime got

into her sweet little gait and they moved

toward the little white darting thing.

Zoom! Out it came, the little white darting
thing. It crossed their path into and under a
bush. Mr. B still couldn't tell what it was.
He and Doubletime moved up a little bit closer.
Zoom! Out it darted again!
But this time, Mr. B saw it!

"Why, it's just a little puppy!
It's just a little white puppy running
scared out here all alone with no mama."
He watched as the puppy disappeared
in the distance. Mr. B said to Doubletime,
"We better not go after it anymore,
Doubletime. If we do, we will just scare it
away. It needs our help out here,
all alone with no mama.
Let's go home and get him some food.
He's bound to need food by now!"

So, off they went toward home.

When he got home, Mr. B looked all
through his pantry to see what he had
that he could make into puppy food—
crackers soaked in milk, anything that he
thought the little puppy might eat.
Then he packed up the food,
got back up on Doubletime
and off they rode again to see if
they could find the little lost puppy.

Well, Mr. B and Doubletime rode
on the levee for a long, long time.
They looked and looked but they couldn't
find the little puppy. Mr. B left the food out
anyway, right where he last saw the puppy.
He hoped the puppy would come and eat it.
Afterwards, he and Doubletime went on home.

For the next few days, Mr. B and Doubletime
rode on the levee among the cows just
as usual, twice a day, every day.
And every now and then, they would see the
little white puppy way up ahead, running among
the cows. But the puppy never let Mr. B and
Doubletime get near to him. He just ran away.
Mr. B kept leaving the food out anyway,
every day, twice a day, because
he knew the puppy needed it.

But the puppy never ate the food.

Weeks went by and winter was beginning to come in the countryside. The winters in the countryside were very rainy and cold. Mr. B was beginning to be very worried for the little puppy, wondering if he would survive. But he knew that he had done all that he could for it.

Mr. B's friends at the farm had seen the little puppy too, on their way to work. As they drove along the old country road, they could see the little puppy scampering along the levee with Mr. B's cows and their new born calves.

Even though he seemed to be getting a little bit bigger, no one knew how the puppy was growing with no food. And everyone, townspeople, friends, and all, were very concerned for him.

One day, Mr. B. was visiting with his friends at the farm house. He told them all about what he had done for the little puppy.
He felt that he had done all he could. His friends all agreed with him. Then, they all just sat together for a while, thinking about what might become of the little puppy.

Then, Mr. B went on his way.

This time, he was driving his old blue pickup truck he named Bessie. Bessie bumped Mr. B all up and down on his seat as he drove down the country road toward the levee. He drove Bessie up on the levee to the barbed wire gap. He opened it and drove right through. He wanted to drive along the top of the levee again to see his cows with their calves and maybe even see the little puppy again.

It was raining. It was getting cold. Mr. B had on his poncho to keep the rain off his face. He was looking straight ahead. Suddenly he saw something he couldn't believe. He stopped Bessie, put on her brake and very quietly got out of her. Then he carefully walked around toward what he thought he saw.

There before him was the puppy
standing up on his hind legs, reaching up
underneath a mama cow, nursing from her milk
bag...like he'd seen the little baby calves do!!
Why, Mr. B couldn't believe it!!! But there was
the little puppy drinking from the only lunch
counter he could find—a mama cow!
And the mama cow didn't mind it at all.
She just stood perfectly still and let her
little friend drink her milk, just like her own
baby calf did, till his heart's content.

Well, what a miracle this was!!! Mr. B was so happy that he jumped right back into Bessie, turned her around and down the levee he drove! He opened the gap and drove right through it. He carefully closed it behind him so as not to let the cows get out. He drove straight to the farm house, knocked on the door, marched right in and shouted the good news to his friends. "The puppy has found a way! The puppy has found a way! He is going to be alright!!" Then he told them all about the little miracle he had just seen. And what wonderful news it was for All!!

All Mr. B's friends were so happy! They ran out to the country road to look over the barbed wire fence to see the little miracle puppy.

And there he was! Not only was he snow white, but when he turned his head around to face them, they could see that he had little black markings all around his eyes and ears.

He looked like he had little patches on him.

So, they called the little puppy Patches.

And Patches was the town hero.

Soon Patches became a legend on the levee and grew to be big and strong. He stayed with Mr. B's herd of cows and never left them, shepherding them to and fro, from pasture to pasture. He kept watch over them.

When the mama cows gave birth to their calves, Patches would stand guard over the mama cow until the calf was born.

Patches then guarded the new born calf until it was strong enough to walk on its own.

The story of Patches grew far and wide,

throughout the whole countryside.

Everyone heard about him and came

to the levee to see the little miracle dog

who had so lovingly adopted this

herd of cows that had so kindly saved his life.

The strangest thing of all is that no one
has ever seen Patches eat dog food,
and no one has ever heard him bark.
So, people still wonder to this day...
Does Patches know he is a dog,
or does he think he is a cow?
Who knows? Only Patches knows.

The End

Patches the Cow Dog is based on a true story.

ELIZABETH I. ACREE has been a published freelance writer for over fifteen years. Her essays and articles have been published in *The Christian Science Monitor*, *The Hollywood Reporter* and in numerous regional publications. She has recently published a coming of age novella, *Liza's World*, available on Amazon and Goodreads. Her further work can be found at elizabethiacreewriting.com. She lives in North Carolina. This is her first children's book.

NANCY NEHLS NELSON is a self-taught oil painter. Originally from the Midwest, she came to the mountains of Western North Carolina in the early 2000s to paint the quiet, simple scenes that surrounded her new home. She was a long-time member of the popular Weaverville Art Safari. She works in a ridgetop studio in the Reems Creek Valley outside of Asheville. Since 2014, she has taught painting at the UNCA College for Seniors. This is the first book she has illustrated.

Made in the USA
Columbia, SC
28 August 2024